BARACK OBAMA'S INAUGURAL ADDRESS

TAMRA ORR

CHERRY LAKE PRESS

Published in the United States of America by Cherry Lake Publishing Group
Ann Arbor, Michigan
www.cherrylakepublishing.com

Reading Adviser: Marla Conn, MS, Ed., Literacy specialist, Read-Ability, Inc.
Content Adviser: Adam Fulton Johnson, PhD, Assistant Professor, History, Philosophy, and Sociology
    of Science, Michigan State University
Photo credits: © Joseph Sohm/Shutterstock.com, cover; © UPI/Alamy Stock Photo, 5; © Eliyahu Yosef
    Parypa/Shutterstock.com, 6; © Everett Historical/Shutterstock.com, 8; © Courtesy Barack Obama
    Presidential Library, 11, 12, 14, 15, 16, 19, 20, 21, 22, 26, 28 [top], 28 [bottom], 29 [top], 29 [bottom];
    © White House Photo/Alamy Stock Photo, 25

Cherry Lake Press is an imprint of Cherry Lake Publishing Group.

Library of Congress Cataloging-in-Publication Data
Names: Orr, Tamra, author.
Title: Barack Obama's inaugural address / Tamra Orr.
Description: Ann Arbor, Michigan : Cherry Lake Publishing, 2021. | Series: Front seat of history: famous
    speeches | Includes index. | Audience: Grades 4-6
Identifiers: LCCN 2020005532 (print) | LCCN 2020005533 (ebook) | ISBN 9781534168831 (hardcover) |
    ISBN 9781534170513 (paperback) | ISBN 9781534172357 (pdf) | ISBN 9781534174191 (ebook)
Subjects: LCSH: Obama, Barack—Inauguration, 2009—Juvenile literature. | Obama, Barack. Inaugural
    address, 2009—Juvenile literature.
Classification: LCC E907 .O77 2020 (print) | LCC E907 (ebook) | DDC 973.932092—dc23
LC record available at https://lccn.loc.gov/2020005532
LC ebook record available at https://lccn.loc.gov/2020005533

Cherry Lake Publishing Group would like to acknowledge the work of the Partnership for 21st Century
Learning, a Network of Battelle for Kids. Please visit http://www.battelleforkids.org/networks/p21
for more information.

Printed in the United States of America
Corporate Graphics

ABOUT THE AUTHOR

Tamra Orr is the author of more than 500 nonfiction books for readers of all ages. A graduate
of Ball State University, she now lives in the Pacific Northwest with her family. When she isn't
writing books, she is either camping, reading or on the computer researching the latest topics.

TABLE OF CONTENTS

CHAPTER 1

The Long Wait

On a cold January day in 2009, almost 2 million people showed up to witness the swearing-in of the United States' first African American president. It felt like a turning point for the nation. It filled many people with renewed hope for the future. As Barack Obama was sworn in, he was joined on the platform by his wife, Michelle Obama, the new First Lady, and the couple's two daughters, 10-year-old Malia and 7-year-old Natasha (Sasha). The Obamas would face many challenges during their 8 years in the White House, but throughout it all, they were a strong family that many admired.

Barack Obama was sworn in as the 44th president of the United States.

The chilly breeze of the January afternoon nipped at Tia's ears. She pulled at her hat. She stood next to her mother and sister. They were a part of the huge crowd at the National Mall in Washington, DC. They were there to watch Barack Obama be sworn in as president.

American flags were waved during President Obama's swearing-in.

"How many people do you think are here?" Tia asked her older sister. Jayden shrugged and went back to looking through the binoculars.

"Look at Malia's bright blue coat," Jayden said to Tia. "I love that color!"

"Is Sasha's coat pink or orange?" Tia asked, trying to see above and around the people in front of her.

"A little of both, I think," replied Mrs. Jefferson. "They sure are patient girls. I bet this day feels like it's never going to end."

A number of people performed and spoke before the swearing-in ceremony began. Just before noon, Chief Justice John Roberts began speaking. As Michelle Obama held the Bible, her husband took the Oath of Office. Tia cheered along with the crowd. The sound of people clapping was muffled because everyone was wearing gloves or mittens.

Around 250,000 people attended the March on Washington
for Jobs and Freedom in 1963.

Tia wondered if Malia and Sasha were excited about their dad becoming president. She thought it would not be as fun and easy as some might think. It would be hard to always be in the **spotlight**.

There was a sudden hush as the new president walked up to the podium. Tia heard her mother take a deep breath. This was the moment they had all been waiting for.

Special Day for a Poet

Before Obama was sworn in, a number of celebrities and others performed, including Yo-Yo Ma, Itzhak Perlman, Aretha Franklin, and poet Elizabeth Alexander. Alexander recited her poem "Praise Song for the Day," which she had written for the occasion. She brought one guest to sit onstage next to her—her father. He wore a large button he had gotten back in 1963 during the March on Washington for Jobs and Freedom. The march was in protest of the challenges and injustices African Americans faced. It was also where Dr. Martin Luther King Jr. delivered his "I Have a Dream" speech. To be at the **inauguration** *of America's first African American president was a moment Alexander and her father would never forget.*

CHAPTER 2

"Hope Over Fear"

"**M**y fellow citizens," the new president began, "I stand here today humbled by the task before us, grateful for the trust you've bestowed, mindful of the sacrifices borne by our ancestors."

Tia expected President Barack Obama to first talk about how wonderful America was, but to her surprise, he took the speech in a different direction. "That we are in the midst of crisis is now well understood," he stated. "Our nation is at war against a far-reaching network of violence and hatred. Our economy is badly weakened."

"Homes have been lost, jobs shed, businesses shuttered," the president said. "Less measurable, but not less profound, is a sapping of confidence across our land; a nagging fear that America's decline is **inevitable**."

The president and first lady dance during the Inaugural Ball.

The Dalai Lama met with President Obama in 2016.

"This doesn't sound like a very happy speech," said Tia.

"Just wait," replied Mrs. Jefferson.

Then Obama changed his tone. "Today I say to you that the challenges we face are real. They are serious and they are many. They will not be met easily or in a short span of time. But know this, America: They will be met. On this day, we gather because we have chosen hope over fear, unity of purpose over conflict and **discord**."

Tia shivered. It was so cold she could see his breath as he spoke. Obama continued by saying that it was "the risk-takers, the doers, the makers of things" who made the biggest differences in the world. He said their example must still be followed today. "Our time of standing pat" was over, he continued. "Starting today, we must pick ourselves up, dust ourselves off, and begin again the work of remaking America."

Mrs. Jefferson muttered a quiet agreement. Tia and Jayden could see why this new president was already so popular. He seemed to understand what people needed to hear. Next, he talked about improving the economy and expanding scientific research.

"How in the world is one **administration** going to accomplish all these things?" someone near Tia muttered.

"What about the war in the Middle East?" someone else asked.

"And our broken health care system," a woman snapped.

President Obama speaks with Ruby Bridges in front of a painting depicting Ruby as a child on the way to her all-white public school.

"Don't forget climate change!" another chimed.

"He's only one man," Mrs. Jefferson whispered.

Obama stood firm. If he could hear the people's doubts, he let them bounce off him. Tia noticed him stand a little taller before he said, "There are some who question the scale of our ambitions, who suggest that our system cannot tolerate too many big plans. Their memories are short, for they have forgotten what this country has already done, what free men and women can achieve when imagination is joined to common purpose, and necessity

In 2012, President Obama sat on the Rosa Parks Bus
at the Henry Ford Museum.

APPROVED

MAR 2 3 2010

The Affordable Care Act was signed into law by President Obama.
He used 22 different pens.

to courage. What the **cynics** fail to understand is that the ground has shifted beneath them, that the stale political arguments that have consumed us for so long no longer apply."

Tia and Jayden kept passing the binoculars back and forth so they could see the president and his family. Jayden was tired of standing and shook out the pain in her feet. She smiled when she saw Malia doing the same thing onstage.

Obama then spoke of the importance of maintaining strong relationships with other countries. "And so, to all the other peoples and governments who are watching today, from the grandest capitals to the small village where my father was born, know that America is a friend of each nation, and every man, woman, and child who seeks a future of peace and dignity. And we are ready to lead once more."

The Nobel Peace Prize

On December 10, 2009, the Nobel Peace Prize was awarded to President Obama. The prize, which has been given out since 1901, is typically given to individuals or to organizations such as the Red Cross. Obama earned it for "his extraordinary efforts to strengthen international diplomacy and cooperation between peoples." In accepting the award, the president stated, "I receive this honor with deep gratitude and great humility. It is an award that speaks to our highest **aspirations***—that for all the cruelty and hardship of our world, we are not mere prisoners of fate. Our actions matter and can bend history in the direction of justice."*

CHAPTER 3

"A Most Sacred Oath"

Tia had to admit that being at this inauguration was more fun than she had expected. She hoped that Sasha and Malia were having fun too.

Just then, President Barack Obama said, "For we know that our patchwork heritage is a strength, not a weakness. We are a nation of Christians and Muslims, Jews and Hindus, and non-believers. We are shaped by every language and culture."

"It's nice that everyone is included," Mrs. Jefferson said quietly.

"The world has changed, and we must change with it," continued Obama. He took a moment to honor people in the military as "the guardians of our liberty." He encouraged everyone

During her time at the White House, First Lady Michelle Obama promoted healthier lunches and higher nutrition standards at schools.

listening to do their part to make the country a kinder, better place. "It is the firefighter's courage to storm a stairway filled with smoke, but also a parent's willingness to nurture a child that finally decides our fate," he explained. He pointed out that the values of honesty, hard work, courage, fairness, tolerance, curiosity, loyalty, and **patriotism** have been "the quiet force of progress throughout our history" and needed to be applied again and again.

In 2016, a video went viral of 106-year-old Virginia McLaurin dancing with the president and first lady in celebration of Black History Month.

These "truths," as Obama called them, were the reason why "a man whose father less than 60 years ago might not have been served in a local restaurant can now stand before you to take a most sacred oath," he said.

This time, the applause exploded with the cheers and shouts of thousands and thousands of Americans. "I bet they could hear that all the way back home," Jayden said to Tia.

The Obama family loves to volunteer together.

First Lady Michelle Obama visited the Great Wall of China
with Sasha and Malia in 2014.

President Obama continued. "America . . . Let it be said by our children's children that when we were tested, we refused to let this journey end, that we did not turn back nor did we falter; and with eyes fixed on the horizon and God's grace upon us, we carried forth that great gift of freedom and delivered it safely to future generations."

Obama finished his speech, stepped back, and smiled. Sasha flashed him a thumbs-up to let him know he did a good job. His smile widened in return. Tia watched as he reached out and kissed both of his daughters and his wife.

"It's going to be a good 4 years," said Jayden confidently.

"Maybe even 8 years," Mrs. Jefferson added with a grin.

Their First Night

Following Obama's inauguration, the president and first lady went to no less than 10 formal parties across Washington. In the meantime, Malia and Sasha had a fun night in the White House. The staff arranged a **scavenger hunt** *for the sisters and their guests. This way, they could have a good time while learning the layout of their new home, including secret passageways and hidden doors. When the sisters got to the final clue, they were surprised to find a musical group waiting for them: the Jonas Brothers. The band played three songs for the girls and their friends, and everyone posed for lots of photos.*

CHAPTER 4

Another Four Years

This time, Tia was ready. She had her own set of binoculars. It had been 4 years since she had stood in the cold with her mom and sister, watching as Barack Obama was sworn in as the 44th president of the United States. Now, here they were again, counting the minutes until he would be sworn in again for a second term.

"Oooooh, look at their purple coats!" Jayden squealed as the two "first daughters" came onto the stage with their grandmother, Marian Robinson. Malia's coat was bright violet, while Sasha's was deep lavender.

In 2013, President Barack Obama was sworn in during his second inauguration.

"They look so much older," said Tia, unaware that she and her sister had grown up just as much during that time.

Tia couldn't help but think of all that had happened over the past 4 years. She was in seventh grade now, far from the little third grader she had been before. Jayden was in high school, and she made sure that everyone around her knew it.

President Obama once said, "Change does not come from Washington, but to Washington."

"I have to wonder what the next 4 years will bring," Jayden said.

"Based on what we've seen for the last 4 years, I feel pretty confident," replied Mrs. Jefferson.

Just then, President Obama started his second inaugural address. "Each time we gather to inaugurate a president, we bear witness to the enduring strength of our Constitution," he began. "We affirm the promise of our democracy. We recall that what binds this nation together is not the colors of our skin or the tenets of our faith or the origins of our names. What makes us

[21ST CENTURY SKILLS LIBRARY]

exceptional—what makes us American—is our **allegiance** to an idea **articulated** in a declaration made more than 2 centuries ago: 'We hold these truths to be self-evident, that all men are created equal; that they are endowed by their Creator with certain unalienable rights; that among these are life, liberty, and the pursuit of happiness.'"

As he spoke, Tia and Jayden watched Malia's and Sasha's faces. It was clear they were very proud of their father. Tia looked forward to the next 4 years. She was sure they would be great.

Their Last Night

On Sasha and Malia's last night in the White House in January 2017, they had pizza and a slumber party. Now 15 and 18 years old, the two were long used to being in the spotlight. They had spent the last 8 years traveling the world with their parents, while still going to school.

1998
Malia Ann is born.

1995
Obama publishes *Dreams from My Father: A Story of Race and Inheritance.*

2004
Obama is elected U.S. senator.

1990

2000

1996
Obama is elected to the Illinois Senate.

2001
Natasha is born.

1992
Barack Obama marries Michelle Robinson.

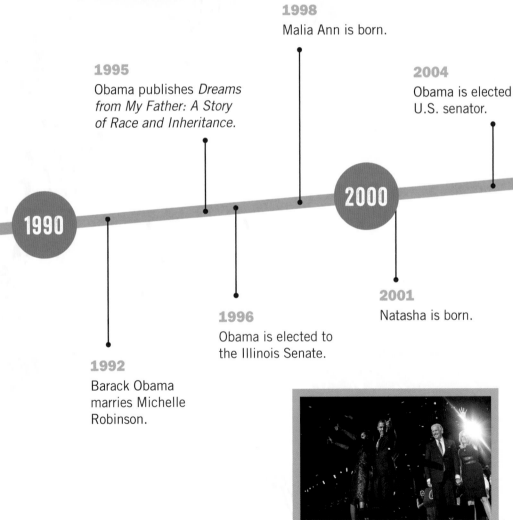

2006
Obama publishes *The Audacity of Hope: Thoughts on Reclaiming the American Dream.*

2009
The Nobel Peace Prize is awarded to President Obama.

2017
Obama finishes his second term as president.

2010

2020

2008
Obama is elected president of the United States.

2012
Obama is reelected president of the United States.

Speech Highlight

"On this day, we gather because we have chosen hope over fear, unity of purpose over conflict and discord. . . . In reaffirming the greatness of our nation, we understand that greatness is never a given. It must be earned. Our journey has never been one of short-cuts or settling for less. It has not been the path for the faint-hearted, for those that prefer leisure over work, or seek only the pleasures of riches and fame. Rather, it has been the risk-takers, the doers, the makers of things—some celebrated, but more often men and women obscure in their labor—who have carried us up the long rugged path toward prosperity and freedom."

Read the full speech at https://obamawhitehouse.archives.gov/blog/2009/01/21/president-barack-obamas-inaugural-address.

Research and Act

Each time new presidents are sworn in, they must give a speech. The speech tells people what directions they plan to take the country in the coming 4 years.

Research
Go to YouTube and find several inauguration addresses. Listen to short sections of each and decide which one you like the most. Then listen to the entire speech and write down the main points the new president is making.

Act
Explain what you liked about the speech and what makes it a good speech. This can be because of what is said, how it is said, who the audience is, and many other factors.

Further Reading

Gilpin, Caroline Crosson. *Barack Obama.* Washington, DC: National Geographic, 2014.

Gormley, Beatrice. *Barack Obama: Our Forty-Fourth President.* New York, NY: Aladdin, 2015.

Souza, Pete. *Dream Big Dreams: Photographs from Barack Obama's Inspiring and Historic Presidency.* New York, NY: Little, Brown and Co., 2017.

GLOSSARY

administration (ad-min-ih-STRAY-shuhn) the government of a president, including the president's cabinet and advisers

allegiance (uh-LEE-juhns) loyal support for someone or something

articulated (ahr-TIK-yuh-lay-tid) expressed clearly

aspirations (as-puh-RAY-shuhnz) desires to achieve something in the future

cynics (SIN-iks) people who always find fault in others and believe the worst will always happen

discord (DIS-kord) disagreement or conflict, especially in a group

inevitable (ih-NEV-ih-tuh-buhl) certain to happen

inauguration (in-aw-gyuh-RAY-shuhn) the ceremony of swearing in a public official, such as a president

patriotism (PAY-tree-uh-tiz-uhm) loyalty to one's country

scavenger hunt (SKAV-uhnj-ur HUHNT) a hunt following clues to find prizes

spotlight (SPAHT-lite) the focus of a lot of public attention

INDEX